This Little Tiger book belongs to:

_____

_____

_____

For Mum and Dad, who put up with my tiny tantrums ~ C C

For Hans Christian, Peder August, Ole Jakob ~ E O

LITTLE TIGER
An imprint of Little Tiger Press Limited
1 Coda Studios, 189 Munster Road, London SW6 6AW
Imported into the EEA by Penguin Random House Ireland,
Morrison Chambers, 32 Nassau Street, Dublin D02 YH68
www.littletiger.co.uk

First published in Great Britain 2017
This edition published 2018
Text copyright © Caroline Crowe 2017
Illustrations copyright © Ella Okstad 2017
Caroline Crowe and Ella Okstad have asserted their rights
to be identified as the author and illustrator of this work
under the Copyright, Designs and Patents Act, 1988
A CIP catalogue record for this book
is available from the British Library
All rights reserved

ISBN 978-1-84869-678-5
LTP/2700/5114/0523
Printed in China
10 9 8 7 6 5

TiNY TaNTRuM

Caroline Crowe

Ella Okstad

LiTTLE TiGER
LONDON

This is **TINY TANTRUM** when she's getting her own way,
Like eating lots of chocolate cake or when it's time to play.

But you try telling Tiny
that she has to
wash heR haiR,

Or tidy up,

or **go to bed,**

and she'll scream,

"THAT'S NOT FAIR!"

Windows **wobble,** jelly **shakes,** and birds **FALL** out of trees,

When Mummy dares to say the words, **"Now, put your coat on please!"**

But one day, just as **TINY** stamped
and screwed her eyes up tight . . .

...a hairy, purple monster gave poor TINY quite a fright!

He said,

"If you don't put your coat on,
    then your bottom will get chilly,

And girls with frozen bottoms
    can't have fun, you SILLY BILLY!"

"YIKES!" she yelled and grabbed her coat,
"Who wants a **chilly bum?**"
She held the monster's furry paw
and followed after Mum.

They **KICKED** through leaves,
and **CLIMBED** up trees,

and **SLID** on icy puddles.

When **TINY** slipped and hurt her knee,
he helped with monster cuddles.

The monster's tummy rumbled so she took him home to eat,
But when she saw the broccoli she stamped her **TINY** feet!

Then over by the cooker, with a chef's hat on his head,
Stood a monster with an apron on,
and this is what he said . . .

"When I eat peas or broccoli,
I do a bottom **wiggle**,

Vegetables taste better
if you eat them
while you
giggle!"

So TINY ate a little bit – she didn't **shout** or **scream**,
And Mummy let them have a bowl of chocolaty ice cream.

At playgroup Molly had the trike so Tiny opened wide.
"I WANT THAT TRIKE, I WANT IT NOW!"
she screamed till Molly cried.

But just as **TINY** tried to snatch,
she heard a whooshing sound.
A monster skidded down the slide
and tumbled to the ground.

He said,

"There are some things that you never share,

like **HICCUPS**, **PANTS** or **SNOT**,

But sharing toys helps make new friends

and keep the ones **you've got.**"

At bedtime **TINY** and her friends
were bouncing on the bed,
When Daddy said that it was time
to brush her teeth instead.

She clenched her fists and **SCREAMED** and **STAMPED**, then, oh what a surprise,

A monster in pyjamas twirled in right before her eyes.

He sang,
"**Brushing teeth's exciting,**
you don't know what you might find –

Some chocolate or a biscuit that got stuck and **left behind!"**

Now **TINY TANTRUM'S** sleepy and she wants to go to bed,
But the monsters are still running round, they want to bounce instead.

"**IT'S TIME FOR SLEEP,**" she says,
but now they screw THEIR eyes up tight ...

"WE don't want to go to bed, we want to **BOUNCE** all night!"

So Tiny says,

"I'LL COUNT TO FIVE,
YOU'D BETTER SHAKE A LEG,

THE LAST ONE IN
AND SNUGGLED DOWN'S
A STINKY, ROTTEN EGG!"

"A stinky egg?!" the monsters cry,
and jump straight into bed,

And TINY plants a goodnight kiss
on every monster's head.

When **Daddy** comes to say goodnight, he doesn't hear a peep. TINY and her **monster friends** are tucked up fast asleep.

Now . . .

...TINY knows the secret and we'll share it with you too –
Don't waste your time on tantrums, sing this song we wrote for you!

"Sometimes things seem boring,
and it makes you want to **SHOUT,**

But don't get cross,
just bend your knees
and **SHAKE** your bum about.

Give yourself a tickle,
flush your tantrum
down the **loo**,

Your grump will go and SOON
you'll get the
MONSTER
giggles
too!"